WITHDRAWN

CITY HORSE

Dodd, Mead & Company · New York

CITY HORSE

By Jack and Patricia Demuth

Our thanks to all the men of Troop E for their cooperation during the many hours we photographed and interviewed, and especially to Sergeant Frank Lewery for his information and good-natured assistance; and to Joni and Jay for printing.

Text copyright © 1979 by Patricia Demuth
Photographs copyright © 1979 by Jack Demuth

1 2 3 4 5 6 7 8 9 10

Library of Congress Cataloging in Publication Data

Demuth, Jack.
  City horse.
  SUMMARY: Photos and text depict the career of one
of the 83 horses of the Mounted Unit of the New York
City Police Department.
  1. Police horses—New York (City)—Juvenile litera-
ture. [1. Police horses. 2. Horses] I. Demuth,
Patricia, joint author. II. Title.
HV7957.D45   363.2   78–23651
ISBN 0–396–07650–5

For Daniel, our son, and Mary Wood, our friend

1

A HORSE NAMED HANNON

New York City is a strange place for a horse to live. But that is Hannon's home—the largest city in the United States.

Hannon is a police horse. His work brings him into the middle of dizzying city turmoil. Trucks roar by him. Bicyclists speed past. Sirens scream. Cars crowd the streets and pedestrians pack the sidewalks. Through it all, Hannon must remain calm.

That's a tall order because horses are by nature sensitive to their environment. They are easily spooked. Hannon is young, just five and a half years old, and he has been in the city only a year and a half, so it is especially hard for him to ignore the commotion that surrounds him. Yet, like the eighty-two other police horses who work for the Mounted Unit of the New York City Police Department, Hannon is able to keep cool as he

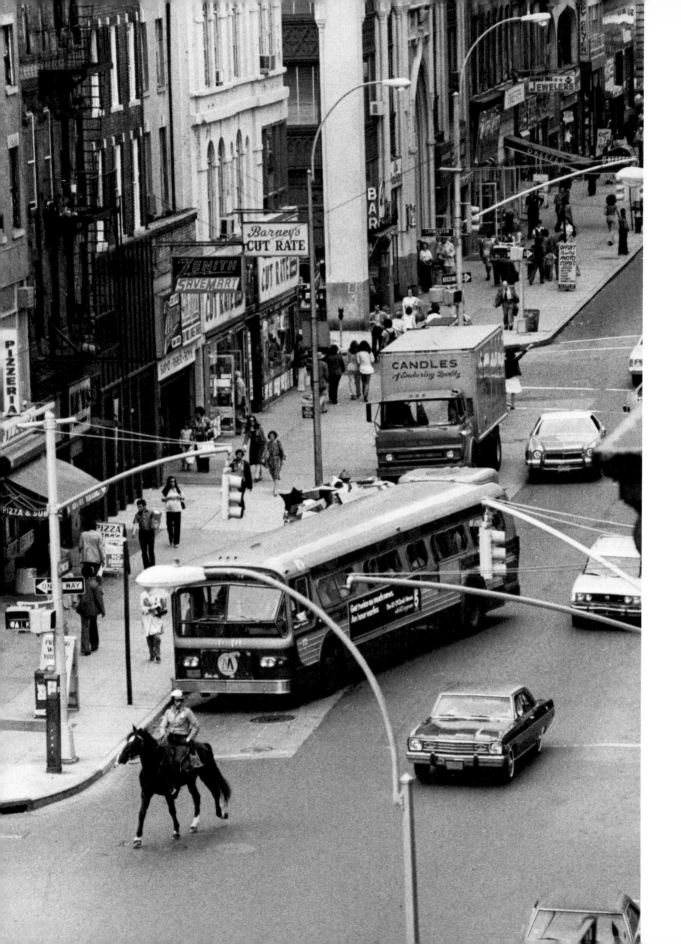

escorts a parade, patrols a crowded beach, cuts a mob in half, chases a suspect, or simply stands in the midst of traffic and watches the bustle and confusion of city life.

He wasn't always a city horse. Hannon was born in the green rolling hills of Tennessee on a huge ranch near Shelbyville. Year round he lived in the open pasture with over one hundred horses, grazing for his food.

Every horse on the ranch was a Tennessee Walker, a breed developed in the South for plantation owners who needed a mount that could carry them comfortably and rapidly over long distances each day. The Tennessee Walker with its inbred running walk—a quick, smooth gait that replaces the jarring trot of most breeds—was the perfect solution.

Tennessee Walkers are known as the "gentlemen among horses," and Hannon was bred for show. Like his father, a show horse named Triple Threat Again, Hannon began his schooling at age two. He was given a rigorous, sometimes harsh, training with the crop. He learned to accept a saddle and rider. Repeatedly he was drilled in the show gaits of the Tennessee Walker: the flat-footed walk, running walk, and canter. He was taught a special show stance.

Then one day when he was four, his life changed—suddenly and drastically. A man from Texas named H. Ross Perot read a newspaper article about money problems in the New York City

Mike and Hannon on their post along Court Street in downtown Brooklyn.

Police Department. Alongside the article was a picture of a poster with a horse's mug shot in the center. It said, "WANTED by the New York City Police Department: HORSES." They could not afford to buy horses for their Mounted Unit.

On his visits to New York, Perot had loved seeing policemen on horses. "That to me *is* New York," he said. So, he decided to buy twenty of the horses on Hannon's ranch and donate them to the department. Up to then, all their police horses were from a hardy, reliable mixed-breed stock. Now, for the first time, purebred Walkers would be on the force. No one knew how they would work out.

In January, 1977, Hannon and the other Walkers stumbled

Mike and Hannon keep sharp eyes out.

out of their nine-horse vans, weak and road-weary from the trip north. Nine hundred miles from home, Hannon smelled gas fumes and winter air for the first time. In a couple days he would try to get his footing on hard, potholed pavement—a surface he had never walked on before. Even the smell of straw bedding in the stable was new to him. In fact, nothing was familiar except the other Tennessee horses.

All the Walkers were sent to Troop E in Brooklyn, one of the five boroughs of New York. There they were tested for three months to see if they were fit for police work. Two officers were put in charge of exposing the Walkers to the city and scoring their responses.

Sergeant Lewery in his office at the Troop E stable.

It was doubtful during the testing period whether Hannon could handle the city. Everything seemed to unnerve him and he would often rear as the officers in charge of testing rode him on the streets. Nine of the Walkers were not kept because they were too high-strung for the city. Hannon almost became number ten. Police officer Mike Sicignano is probably the one who changed that.

Mike went to look over the Walkers the day they arrived. Mounted policemen in New York are allowed to choose their horses, and Mike was due for a new one. His former mount had been given to a sergeant when Mike was laid off the Mounted Unit for a couple months because of budget cuts.

Mike and Hannon hit it off beautifully from the start. "I walked into his stall and he put his nose into my pocket," says Mike. "I knew he was somebody's puppy."

Hannon's good looks also appealed to Mike. "The white socks, the white forehead—these are things I like." So, impulsively, he requested Hannon.

Other officers rode two or three horses on the streets before making their choice, but Mike never worried about his decision. Even the bad reputation Hannon developed didn't scare him. He was willing to work hard to train him. "The other men didn't want Hannon because he reared a lot and was generally

A tight squeeze during afternoon rush hour can make Mike nervous because drivers may not see his horse. But Hannon pays no attention to the crowded traffic he freely passes by.

ornery," Mike says. "I learned to understand him. He's a piece of cake."

Mike and Hannon go well together. Hannon is by nature spirited, happiest when he's moving, discontent when he must stand long in one place. Mike is active, too. Easily bored, he likes a change of scene. If Hannon gets restless on the streets and paws at the pavement, Mike understands and walks him for a couple blocks. Satisfied to be on the go, Hannon threads his way through traffic like a skier on a slalom course.

Mike understands, too, that Hannon has not been away from Tennessee very long and still needs time to adjust. Mike gives in when he can. He lets Hannon, a natural grazer, nibble at a lawn or poke around in a garbage can full of temptations. He

This truck once hauled hay. Hannon caught a whiff of his favorite scent and couldn't resist nibbling the sweet-smelling wood.

lets him waltz over to things that catch his curiosity—anything from trucks to baby carriages.

Mike admits he pampers Hannon. "I let him get away with things. I'm very lenient. Most guys wouldn't take what he does," he says, referring to Hannon's shows of impatience. Some riders prefer a calmer horse than Hannon, but a placid horse would simply bore Mike. Since it is essential that police horses and their riders get along well during the long hours they spend together, it is fortunate that Mike enjoys Hannon's personality.

And Hannon appreciates Mike. As they stand together on the street, he affectionately nuzzles Mike's hand or rubs his forehead on Mike's arm. He invites Mike to play by nipping

After making sure the garbage was safe, Mike let his scavenger horse finish a lettuce-and-bread sandwich. Horses are herbivorous.

Time out . . .

to goof around . . .

and laugh.

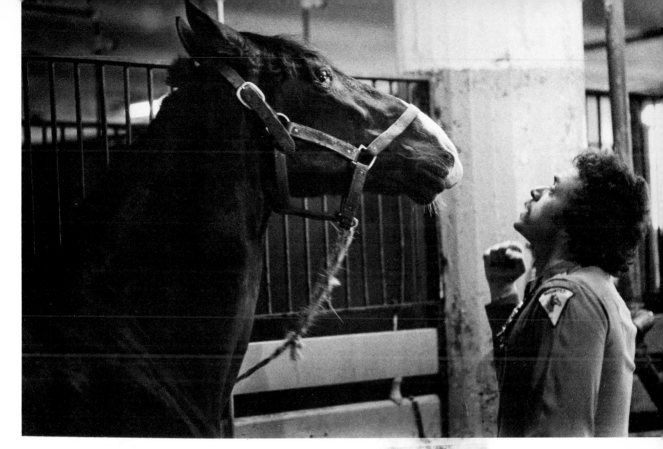

Hannon would not stay in position to be saddled, but when he realized Mike was in no mood for games, he settled down.

or pushing his shoulder. Then Mike elbows back, and the pair head and arm wrestle like two playful kids. "I almost picked another horse, McDermott," Mike says of another Walker on the force. "But Hannon has a better personality. You can play with him—you can't do that with McDermott."

It's not always fun and games, of course. Even best friends can get on each other's nerves. Sometimes Hannon won't settle down and then Mike gets stern. He may even shout or shake a fist at him in frustration. In a couple minutes, though, it's forgotten.

"You can always tell the best horses," says Al Reese, a stable hand at Troop E. "They have riders who really care for them."

17

2

LIFE ON THE JOB

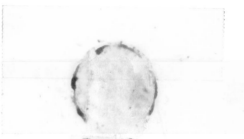

It's a typical night at Coney Island Amusement Park in Brooklyn—wild and weird. People shriek and scream as they are whirled, whizzed, tossed, and thrown by an assortment of nerve-jangling rides. Spooky groans and the hollow sound of recorded laughter reverberate from the Fun House. Highways of light stretch in every direction. A barker shouts, "Over here, Miss! Win a big prize, Miss!" Still seventy degrees at ten o'clock, the hot summer night is unrelieved by breezes from the Atlantic Ocean at the park's edge.

Thousands of people mill around. That is why Hannon and Mike, as well as another officer and his mount, are stationed here. Wherever there are crowds of people, there is the opportunity for trouble.

19

Hannon and Mike walk their beat in Coney Island.

At this hour, Coney Island is nothing *but* trouble for Hannon. Added to all the unsettling sights and sounds, the shrill music of the merry-go-round has just started to blare, and a subway train rumbles overhead. Hannon is jumpy and nervous. Coney Island, strange enough to a person, must be positively eerie to a horse, and this assignment is Hannon's roughest. At other posts he is friendly, even outgoing. But at Coney Island Mike won't let people near him.

It is Hannon's first summer working at Coney Island. "I

*Hannon rarely rears any more, but the Zipper's
sudden start was more than he could take.*

*At Coney Island Amusement Park, Mike picked up a call to be on the
lookout for "a man trying to pick fights with the carnies." But
Mike never spotted him and there were no more complaints.*

expect him to be much more mellow in a few months," says
Mike, who has seen Hannon adapt beautifully to other posts
that were also scary at first. At the end of two years Hannon will
have worked all of Troop E's routine assignments.

Troop E is Brooklyn's only troop of mounted policemen. It
is small: Sergeant Lewery at the head, seven working men, and
eight troop horses. Women haven't worked in the Mounted
since 1975, when large numbers of officers were laid off the
unit.

Headquarters assigns Troop E to a variety of posts on the day
and night shifts. The men and their mounts may be sent to

With the rest of Troop E, Mike and Hannon stand guard as the St. Patrick's Day parade marches down Fifth Avenue. The previous year mounted men had to break up a rioting mob.

trouble spots that flare up unexpectedly in Brooklyn. They may be called into Manhattan, the center of New York City, to help out Troop A at a strike, demonstration, parade, or rock concert. But they usually patrol two of Brooklyn's busiest areas—downtown Brooklyn and the business district of Brighton Beach. In summer they are also assigned to Coney Island and Brooklyn's packed Atlantic beaches.

These areas are heavily populated and mounted men are there to make citizens feel safe. More importantly, they are there to prevent crime before it occurs. How? By being highly visible.

Mike and Hannon patrol Manhattan Beach on a scorching summer day. During the shift, Mike will wade Hannon in the cool Atlantic to avoid heat prostration.

Mike and Hannon . . .

keep onlookers out . . .

of a marital dispute.

A view from Hannon's back.

Hannon is sixteen and a half hands high—that's five feet six inches. Atop Hannon, Mike is ten feet tall; his knees are above the roofs of most cars. Anyone planning trouble cannot help but be aware of him. "A guy out there who's ready to pull a stunt, he sees a mounted man and he knows his horse can move fast," says Sergeant Lewery. "The guy thinks, 'I'm not gonna take a chance. I'll take my business elsewhere. There's plenty of pickings in this town.'"

A horse and rider are a change of scene on a New York City beach.

A twelve-hundred-pound horse and a rider with a loaded gun are an intimidating pair, indeed. And if trouble does start or an emergency does arise, Mike and Hannon can get there in an instant. Unlike a patrol car, Hannon can weave through sunbathers, crowded streets, or the narrow walkways of an amusement park. Mike and Hannon can pursue a suspect without concern for traffic jams or one-way streets. They can even go up on the sidewalk if necessary.

A policeman on a horse also has advantages in riot and crowd control. "One mounted man can do the job of a dozen foot cops in a riot," says Sergeant Lewery. Hannon and the other horses on the force are trained to sidestep to the left or right.

Hannon rests his foot while standing at a post along Coney Island Avenue. An angry horse may cock his foot the same way when ready to kick.

Their feet move in a crisscross pattern. By sidestepping at the front lines of a crowd, they can gently nudge it backward without anyone realizing what is happening. It's a tactic that can prevent a heated strike or demonstration from going out of control.

If a full-fledged riot does occur, mounted men can cut its power without resorting to violence. In one of their maneuvers, they form a sort of wedge, like flying geese, and head straight into the middle of a mob, splitting it in half.

In the midst of a tense, angry crowd, Mike needs to concentrate fully on the situation at hand. Hannon cannot be part of the problem. A mounted officer must be confident that his horse

In an empty parking lot, Mike practices sidestepping with Hannon, who hasn't had to use this maneuver for a while. When he does it correctly, both left legs cross over at the same time.

will respond quickly to signals, work through the crisis with him, and keep calm regardless of what happens. "At first I was apprehensive with a new horse on the streets," says Mike. "For a few months I was on my guard. Now I can get Hannon to do anything."

But it wasn't always so. Before budget cuts, the New York City police used to give new horses special training. In the safety of a corral, the horses were exposed to stressful situations like the ones they would meet on city streets. Trainers waved balloons in their faces, fired blank bullets near their ears, let off smoke bombs, blared music from loudspeakers, and ran back and forth in front of them like wild men. Hannon did not have any of this preparation. Mike had a reckless rookie on his hands.

The first morning they worked together, Mike and Hannon were in the middle of Times Square. It is one of the busiest, most congested areas of Manhattan, where three main avenues come together. Within minutes, Hannon reared violently and walked up the middle of Forty-second Street on his two hind legs, determined to shake the intruder off his back.

Mike, just as determined, hit Hannon hard on the head with his fist. In doing so, he made Hannon think that he hit himself on the head by rearing. If Mike had yanked on the reins, Han-

Hannon has been restless and Mike is tired.

non would probably have fallen on his back and crushed Mike beneath him.

Mike thinks Hannon was testing him that time, finding out who was boss. Mike won, and Hannon stopped rearing. But plenty of things still frightened him. He was afraid of crosswalk lines, puddles, and sewer plates and would try to jump over them. He balked whenever open-ended trucks rattled by. And he refused to go near overhead umbrellas at hot dog stands.

To break his fear of umbrellas, Mike shoved the crop before Hannon's eyes and forced him to approach one. Hannon did so on sheer nerve.

"He bit out at the umbrella as soon as he was near," said

Overhead umbrellas no longer terrify Hannon.

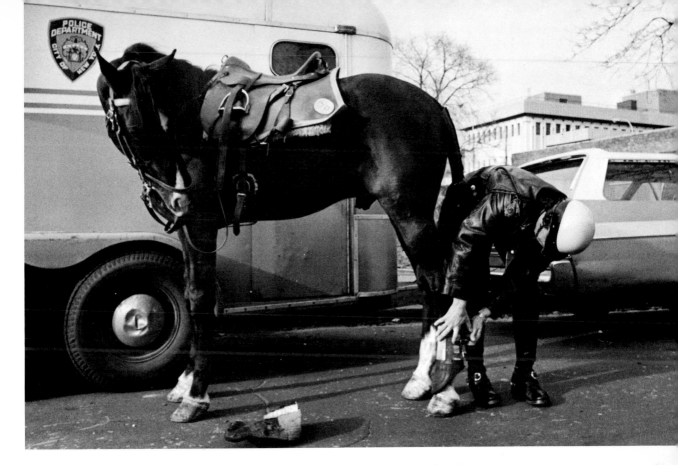

Hannon watches Mike fasten a shipping boot.

Mike. "Then he found it didn't bite him back. The hot dog man gave him one of the frankfurter rolls and Hannon started eating and forgot the whole thing."

Mike never threatens Hannon with his nightstick. "If I did that, Hannon would be afraid whenever he saw it," Mike explains. "I'd have a panicky horse on my hands if I needed to use it. In fact, at first I twirled the stick in front of Hannon's eyes just to get him used to it."

Of course on most days Mike doesn't have to use either the crop or the nightstick. Most days are routine for Mike and Hannon. Unless he is near enough to walk, Hannon travels to the assigned post in a blue and white two-horse van pulled by

Mike secures Hannon's tail wrap.

a police station wagon. Mike puts a tail wrap on Hannon to keep his tail hairs from rubbing off against the van door. He also puts shipping boots on Hannon's legs to keep them from getting cut in case Hannon loses his balance when the van sways and steps on his own feet.

On stormy days when pouring rain makes it hard for drivers to see, Hannon is not allowed on the streets. He stays in the van, on call in case the weather improves, and Mike patrols alone. In winter, if temperatures fall below fifteen degrees, Hannon does not even leave the stable. Otherwise, he and Mike work in all kinds of weather.

When there is heavy rain, Hannon stays warm and dry inside the van.

Two men and their mounts are usually assigned to one post. They often stand guard on different blocks, but whenever the horses see one another, they fidget and paw until their riders give in and let them get together. Despite all the other street life, the horses immediately recognize one of their own kind.

Throughout the shift, Mike keeps an ear tuned to his two-way radio to pick up calls for help. "Past larceny at 110 Court Street. Complainant on the scene. What unit is available?" the voice on the radio will say if someone just robbed a store at 110 Court and got away. If Mike is nearby, he immediately takes off on Hannon, notifying headquarters via radio that he

Mike's radio provides his contact with headquarters. Here, he radios in that a little girl is lost.

is on his way. Another mounted man or patrol car in the area will automatically come to back him up.

Even when they take urgent calls, mounted men are not supposed to gallop their horses on pavement. The danger is too great that the horse will slip and fall on a smooth surface. Says Sergeant Lewery, "We have a standing order that a horse will not be cantered on pavement except in extreme emergencies. Yet when a ten-thirteen comes over the radio, which means a fellow officer is in trouble, I've seen a man canter down Broadway. But all he needs is to hit one manhole cover and down he goes."

Responding to a call about a theft at a delicatessen, Mike and Hannon head down Brighton Beach Avenue.

Mike makes out a parking ticket.

Mike has answered hundreds of calls, including some to break up knife fights, aid heart attack victims, pursue robbers, and calm disorderly persons. But he makes few arrests. A mounted man's job is to stop crime by being highly visible.

Between calls, Mike patrols. Sitting on Hannon, he directs traffic at a jammed corner. He tickets illegally parked cars. He gives lots of directions and answers plenty of questions. He checks out anything that looks suspicious or unusual, such as a gathering crowd or a wrecked car.

Something suspicious-looking is exactly what Mike hopes for

On Hannon's back, Mike is a handy traveling source of information.

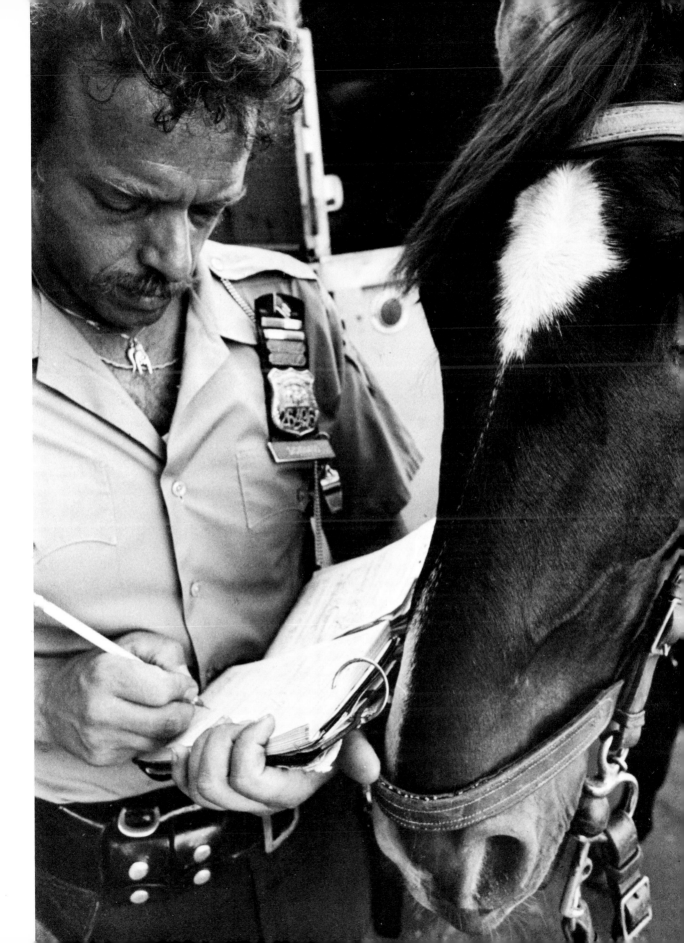

sometimes. Day after day can go by uneventfully. "The biggest enemy on this job is time," says Mike, whose favorite post is Hannon's worst—Coney Island—because it is popping with trouble.

A post that seems boring to Mike can look very different to Hannon, however. He can suddenly be frightened when a fire engine, ambulance, or police car screams past; when a street cleaner with its monstrous rollers gulps the trash at his feet; when construction workers drill nearby; when newspapers and other trash fly through the air like witches; when a bus or truck backfires and horns honk right near his ear.

Serious accidents can happen if a horse shies badly when startled. George Haubold of Troop E will never ride a horse on duty again because of a knee injury he received when his horse shied. "He was Crazy Horse, that guy," Joe says of the mount who was simply too nervous to adjust to the city, even after a year's exposure. "A bus went by and the horse skidded right across the street. A car hit him, threw me over the hood, and I landed on my knee."

Mike believes that Hannon would never shy violently enough to hurt either of them. When he does balk at something, Mike responds immediately, checking the reins or squeezing a knee. Hannon is harder to control when Mike is off his back, and sometimes a sharp rebuke is necessary.

*When Hannon is jumpy on new assignments, Mike may threaten
him with the crop to make him behave. Mike's firm authority actually
helps Hannon perform more confidently and keeps them both safe.*

Periodically Mike dismounts to give Hannon a rest and to give himself a stretch. Still, during a working shift, Hannon carries Mike for about five hours. When you consider that Mike weighs one hundred ninety pounds, his clothing, helmet, gun, radio, and other gear weigh about eleven pounds, and the tack (saddle and riding equipment) weighs thirty-five pounds, you realize Hannon bears quite a load.

Like all horses, Hannon loves to run, and police work doesn't give him much chance. But Hannon is lucky as city horses go. If he and Mike are stationed near the shore, in the cool of the day Mike takes him on a beach as open and free as a Tennessee pasture. Hannon lets loose, his hooves pound along the wet coast of the Atlantic Ocean, his salty mane flies back, his spirits soar.

During Mike's lunch hour (at eight o'clock on the night shift), Hannon stays in a parking lot or a garage. Peculiar things can happen when a horse is "parked." One New York police horse ate half a convertible top off a car for his lunch. Another broke loose and was nowhere in sight when his officer returned to the lot. After the police searched three hours for a runaway horse, the parking attendant found him at the top of the stairs. He had nudged open the door and had simply stood there waiting to be rescued.

*Freedom. Mike gallops Hannon on Coney Island Beach
not far from their post.*

Hannon made a friend when he was parked one day. While Mike was tying Hannon to a post, a ten-year-old boy shyly walked up. He gazed at Hannon through the fence.

"Hello there," said Mike, noticing the boy's wistful face.

"Hi," said the boy. "What's your horse's name?"

"Hannon. You watch him for me while I go eat, okay?" said Mike casually, as he walked off for lunch.

An hour later, Mike returned and was amazed to find the boy still there. He and Hannon had become acquainted over the fence, mostly through silence and gentle forehead rubs.

"What's your name?" Mike asked.

"Michael."

Hannon waited patiently during Mike's lunch hour.

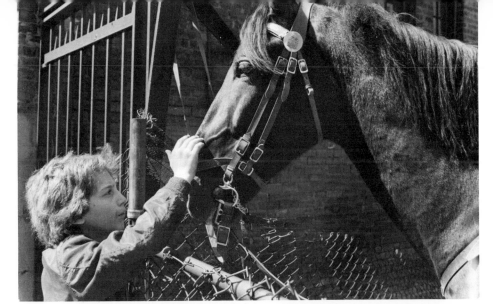

Gentle movements . . .

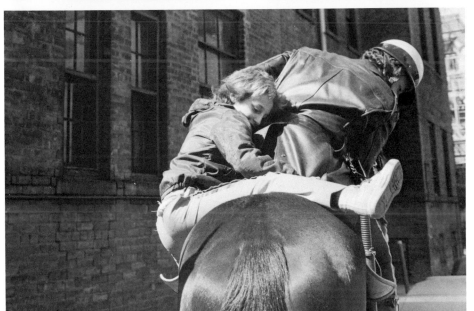

make a friend . . .

of Hannon.

When school is out for the day, Hannon has plenty of attention.
He is the first exposure to a live horse many city children have.

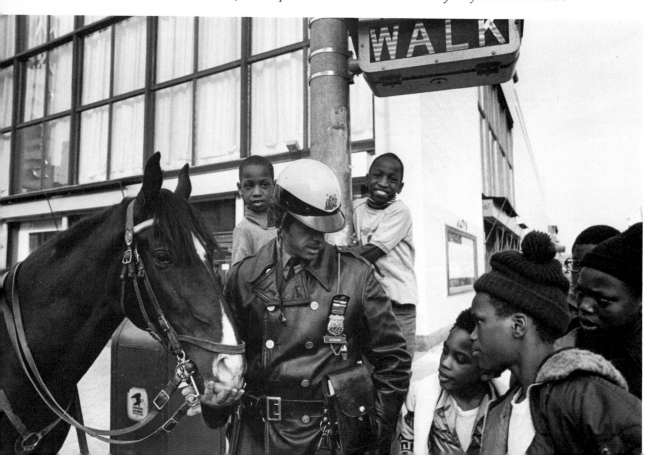

*Hannon is not just saying hello to a surprised little girl—
he is looking for the cookie he smells.*

"Hey, that's my name, too. Hop on, Michael. I'll give you a ride for doing such a good job."

Mike almost never gives rides on Hannon—he would be swamped with requests if he did. But this was an exception, for Michael lives at a home for orphan boys in downtown Brooklyn.

People come up to Mike and Hannon all day long. "What's your horse's name?" they ask. "Will he bite? Can I pet him?"

With children Hannon is remarkably patient. Some fearless youngsters have safely put their hands right in Hannon's

47

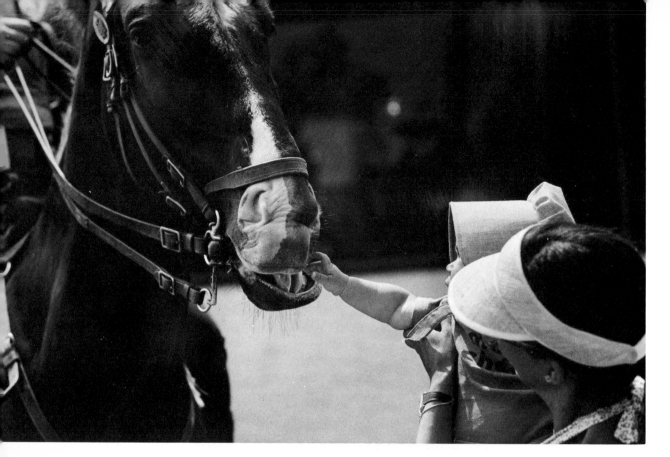

A touch and a sniff express mutual curiosity.

mouth. And Hannon has been known to amble over to a buggy or car with children inside and poke his nose in to say hello.

However, by the end of a working shift, Hannon has had about two hundred hands exploring his head, neck, and legs. Suddenly he may jerk his head and open his mouth as if to nip.

"He's a big phoney," explains Mike. "He'll never bite, but he wants you to think he will."

When it's time to go home, Hannon is probably tired. But you'd never know it from his lively behavior. Perhaps he can fairly feel the peace of his stall. He knows food is waiting for him there. He knows he will be bedded and groomed. He knows he will get the rewards a hard-working horse deserves.

A quiet exchange.

3

HOME LIFE

The Troop E stable is a three-story brick building on a residential street in south Brooklyn. A visitor who opens its ground-floor door suddenly steps out of the city into a country atmosphere. Two dogs, Missy and Jumper, greet any stranger. Missy barks ferociously, trying to protect her five puppies nestled in the third-floor hayloft. Jumper, friend to human and horse alike, will escort any guest past Sergeant Lewery's office to the second floor where the horses are kept.

The stable smells faintly of ammonia mixed with the smell of leather tack and the fresh sweet smell of hay. The stone floor is clean due to the hostlers' daily scrubbing. Saddles and bridles rest on pegs against the wall. When the horses are working, their row of vacant stalls stands like an empty classroom waiting for noisy children to return.

Jumper and Missy and their puppies in the third-floor hayloft.

Hannon's "room" is a stall nine feet long and five feet wide. There are twenty-nine other stalls exactly like his, and one large stall, twelve by twenty feet, for the sergeant's horse. Usually about fifteen stalls are occupied at one time—eight by the troop horses and the remainder by transient horses who come to Troop E for what Sergeant Lewery calls their "R and R," rest and relaxation.

Once frightened of Jumper, Hannon is now friends with him. Jumper got his name when he went out a second-story window after a squirrel.

The stable is quiet when the seven working horses are gone.
Keeping the floor clean is a constant task.

Some people think that a horse should not be cooped up in a stall. Others believe that a horse likes the security a stall provides. In a barn fire, they point out, horses refuse to leave their stalls, forcing people to yank them out by their tails. Hannon seems to like his stall. It is his own space, with his name above the entrance and a window above his head, the place where he receives his food, water, and bedding.

Troop E has five hostlers, stable hands who are in charge of feeding and grooming the horses and keeping the stable clean. They are probably busiest in winter when the horses cannot work because of icy streets and freezing weather. For several days in a row, the horses may stay inside, cloths on their backs

Outside, the streets are icy and the weather freezing, but inside Hannon is warm and dry. Groomed and washed, he'll return to his stall after a drink of water.

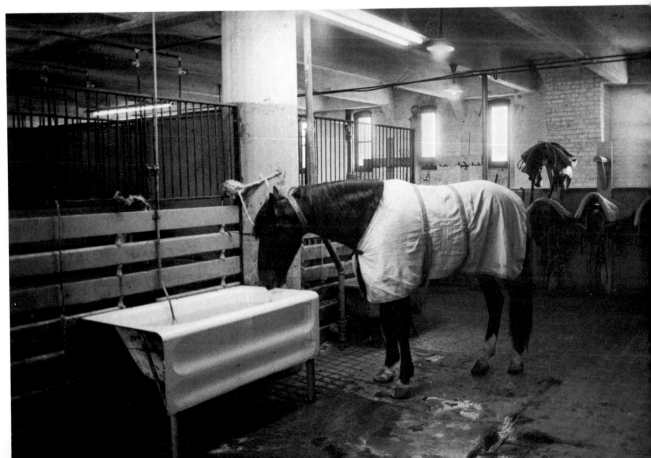

for warmth. Pretty soon some start nipping and kicking out at their "stall mates," disrupting stable harmony. Then the hostlers rearrange the horses, just like teachers moving troublesome students to the back.

Hannon has a love-hate relationship with Apache, the horse in a neighboring stall. When they face forward out of their stalls, as they do when they are saddled and waiting for their riders, Hannon and Apache nip playfully at each other. But then one of them becomes annoyed, and the nipping gets serious. A hostler breaks up the fight, taking one to wait elsewhere.

For exercise, the hostlers turn the horses out to the corral in back—an open space that is one hundred by fifty feet. Troop E is fortunate to have a corral. Some troops in the Mounted Unit have no space to run their horses, and in the wintertime especially, the horses can get colic from lack of exercise. Even when horses are working, they seldom have an opportunity to run unless their officers take them to a nearby beach or park. Exercise is one of the reasons that horses from other troops are sent for a while to Troop E.

Hannon had never seen snow until he was let out in the corral one February morning. He sniffed the air and got a few snowflakes in his nostrils. He shook his mane and ran a few paces. Then he experienced the soft, cold wonder by getting

Sometimes the friendly nipping between Hannon and Apache turns tough, and the hostlers have to separate them before a nose gets cut.

In the Troop E corral, Hannon greets the snow and frisks with another horse.

down on his back and rolling in it. Rolling is an instinctive passion for a horse—a way of self-grooming—and it is the first thing that most horses do when they're let out, no matter what the season.

Once a day the hostlers groom every horse. Hannon and the other working horses are groomed just before they are saddled. Hannon loves it. He stands peacefully and soaks in the vigorous rub of the hard currycomb and the firm strokes of the soft-bristled body brush. Good grooming massages the skin and underlying muscles, helps circulation, and, of course, cleans the horse.

The hostlers feed the horses three times a day, starting at five

Al Reese grooms Hannon's head with a soft-bristled brush. McDermott, the sergeant's horse, is so head-shy that Al must bridle him before he can touch his head.

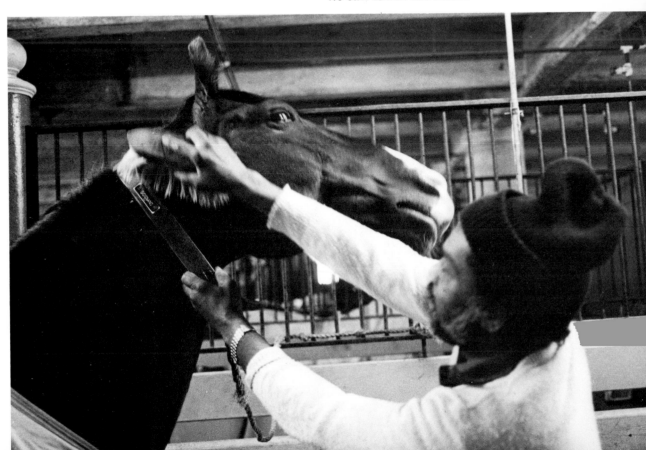

in the morning. In the winter it is still dark then, but Hannon has been awake for half an hour, hungry for his ten pounds of hay. The hostlers get the hay from the third floor of the stable —one giant room, or "hayloft."

At the next feeding, each horse receives five pounds of pellets that the hostlers scoop out of a wheelbarrow with an old coffee can. The horses go wild when they hear the pellet wagon coming. They kick, jump, whinny, whine, and wheel around as far as their ropes allow. The pellets are a high-energy mix of several grains that replaces oats.

At night there is just one hostler on duty. At ten o'clock he gives the horses their last feeding and then forks four pounds of straw into each stall. It will keep the horses dry, warm, and comfortable.

About midnight, the lights are turned out. The moon shines through the stall windows, passing as quietly as the night in the silent stable.

Hannon sleeps, sometimes standing. He may lie down for only two or three hours a night; but he will sleep for about seven hours in all. Horses can sleep standing, and some don't lie down for days at a time.

At dawn, the stable comes alive again.

Unlike Hannon, Mike is not lively in the morning. He stumbles in about 9:40 when he works the day shift. (The

In the morning before tacking up, Mike greets Hannon.

The saddle . . .

the bridle . . .

and Hannon is ready.

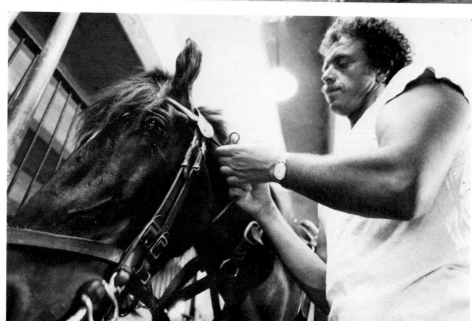

night shift is from four to midnight.) After reviving himself with a cup of coffee and changing into his uniform trousers, Mike greets Hannon with a rub on the forehead. Hannon knows this routine well and rests his head on Mike's shoulder.

Mike leads Hannon to the open area and goes for the tack. A horse's tack is all the equipment used for riding, including saddle, bit, bridle, and cloths.

Several men talk to their horses as they saddle them. It's not Mike's style to chatter in the morning. But he does hum, and Hannon usually offers no resistance as Mike places a cloth on his back, then the leather pad that has the New York City Police Department insignia as well as a slot for Mike's night-

Mike "paints" Hannon's "toenails" with a tar-base solution that helps protect his hooves.

stick. On top of these, Mike centers the saddle. Then he puts the bit in Hannon's mouth and slips the bridle over his head. The tacking-up is over in two minutes.

With a paintbrush, Mike applies a hoof dressing that will keep Hannon's feet from becoming dry and brittle. Mike lifts Hannon's feet and examines them carefully for evidence of thrush, a disease that softens the inner part of the foot and causes lameness. A horse can get thrush from standing in moisture, such as wet straw, or from collecting too much dirt inside the hoof. Before each shift, Mike cleans out Hannon's hooves with a pick.

As a special treat, Mike also brushes Hannon and combs his tail. Then he goes into the locker room with the other officers, leaving Hannon tied outside the door. A small, smoky room filled with cabinets and chairs, the locker room is the place where the men gather to talk and relax.

At exactly 10:10 every morning, Sergeant Lewery calls the roll.

"Sicignano," he says in a firm voice.

"Present," says Mike.

"Post eleven in the six-one. Meal at thirteen hundred. At fourteen hundred post-change to post twelve in the six-one."

Mike scribbles the assignment in his memo book as the sergeant reads. In plain English, his assignment is to go to a

A mounted policeman generally takes pride in his horse's appearance. Mike uses the tail brush to spruce Hannon up, even though the hostlers have just groomed him.

Hannon waits in the hallway while the sergeant calls the roll and gives special instructions for the day.

certain five-block area (post eleven) in the 61st precinct (the six-one). His meal is at 1:00 (thirteen hundred) for one hour. At 2:00 (fourteen hundred) he changes to post twelve in the 61st precinct.

Mike straps his book to his belt, grabs his helmet, and with the other men goes out the door to get his horse. Accustomed to this schedule, Hannon has been expecting Mike right then —at 10:20.

A long ramp leads from Hannon's floor to the ground floor.

One of the transient horses on vacation at the stable looks down at Hannon and Mike going off to work.

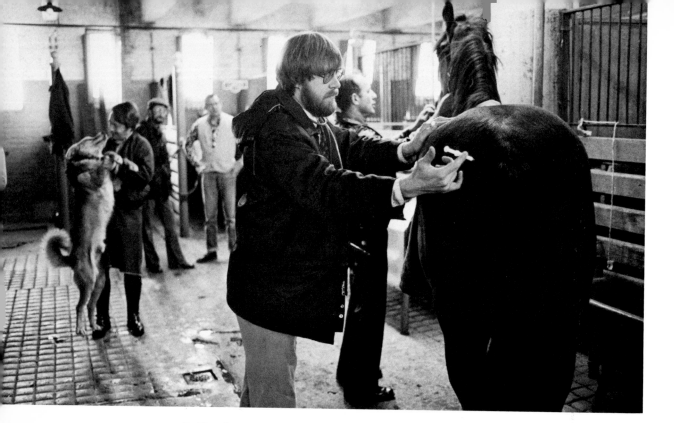

Police horses are innoculated periodically against diseases. Officers stand by to aid in case a horse rears or kicks.

The working horses go down the ramp, and the stable resumes a quietness after the hustle of morning preparations. Only the transient horses are left behind.

Hannon sometimes stays behind too—when the vet comes for a routine checkup. Emil Dolensek, the veterinarian at the Bronx Zoo, is the main vet and consultant for the Mounted. He comes to Troop E periodically to vaccinate the horses for equine influenza, tetanus, and infectious anemia—diseases common to horses. During his visits, Dolensek always checks the horses' eyes to make sure they have normal vision-and-light response. On city streets a horse with impaired vision would be disastrous.

Hannon also stays in the stable when he needs to be shod.

In order to melt iron, the temperature of the coke in Henry's forge must be hotter than 1500° C.

Henry Nixon, the gentle blacksmith who's been working around horses for forty years, quietly leads Hannon to his shop on the ground floor of the stable. The forge, a blacksmith's oven, hisses with fire as they enter.

Horseshoes are everywhere in Henry's shop—in old boxes, hanging on racks, lying on tables and on the floor. Some are rusted, others shiny new, and they come in five sizes. Most horses wear a size three or four, but Hannon has a small foot. He wears size one.

Horses need shoes to cover the hornlike walls at the bottom of their feet. The wall is the part of the hoof you see when the foot is on the ground. If you lift a horse's foot and look at it from the underside, you see that the wall there extends around

69

the edge of the foot in a U shape. A horseshoe is made to fit this shape. In the center, the foot is raised or concave, like an overturned saucer.

Since the wall hits the ground at every step, it takes quite a beating and can be worn away. However, the wall also grows continuously. In the wild, a horse's feet are naturally protected because the wall grows downward and replaces what the ground wears away. But on hard road surfaces, the wall does not grow quickly enough to replace what is being lost. Thus shoes are needed for protection. Once a horse is shod, however, the situation is reversed. The protected wall continues to grow and eventually becomes overlong and requires trimming. Hannon's shoes must be removed and his feet trimmed every four weeks.

Henry fits Hannon with a special type of shoe that is worn by other American police horses. He welds four knobby metal cleats to the bottom of the iron shoe. The cleats help keep Hannon from slipping and sliding on smooth city surfaces.

Crouching, Henry picks up Hannon's huge hind leg and rests it on his thigh. With pliers he pulls off the old shoe and trims the wall with a knife. Hannon doesn't seem to mind. He stares off into space. Like the nails on our fingers and toes, the wall of Hannon's foot has no feeling.

When the trimming is over, Henry files the bottom of the

Henry pulls an old shoe off Hannon. Crouching under a twelve-hundred-pound animal is dangerous, but Henry says a horse can sense right away if you're afraid, and then you can't do anything with him.

Henry files the bottom of Hannon's hoof to make it smooth.

wall to make it smooth. Then he takes a horseshoe, and using tongs, thrusts it into the middle of the intense flames. It is black when it goes in, but within one minute the horseshoe is an angry red and soft enough to be shaped to fit Hannon's foot exactly.

At his anvil, Henry pounds the shoe to make it flat. Sparks fly. He also pounds out a pie-shaped wedge at the curved end of the shoe. Called a "toe clip," it keeps the shoe from slipping once it's on.

Henry needs great strength to handle his job. Here at the anvil, he pounds the hot horseshoe to level it.

Despite the smoke, Hannon doesn't feel a thing. The wall of his foot has no nerves.

Sticking a pick through one of the nail holes, Henry places the shoe on Hannon's foot to check the fit. Smoke pours out. The wall is so thick, however, that Hannon doesn't flinch.

Henry says that not all horses are as patient as Hannon while being shod. "Some horses say 'I don't *want* those shoes, I won't *have* those shoes' and you say 'But you have to have those shoes.'" One police horse kicks at Henry the entire time he tries to shoe him. When the horse is finally shod, he stumbles out of Henry's shop trying to shake the shoes off!

Henry may pound the shoe again if it needs to be made more narrow or wide. Then he dips it, now black, into a bucket of water to cool it. The shoe sizzles as it goes in. "Around here, you don't pick up anything unless you know it's cold," warns

Henry makes small adjustments in the shape of the shoe so that it will fit Hannon's foot exactly.

Henry. "Black heat can be more dangerous than red because you don't see it. You can pick up something hot and it sticks to your hand."

Finally Henry puts the cool shoe in place and pounds four-inch nails through the holes right into the wall of Hannon's foot. After years of experience, he can tell by the sound whether a nail is going in correctly. An unskilled blacksmith can lame a horse by driving the nail into or near the tender area of the foot.

Henry is sixty-four years old, but stronger than most young men. "You have to have a mighty strong back for this job," he says. That's especially true when he gets a tricky horse who leans all his weight on the leg that Henry is holding. Two years

If the nail goes in correctly, it doesn't hurt Hannon.
It enters the bottom of the wall and comes out the side.

ago a horse suddenly decided he didn't want Henry holding his foot. He stepped down and broke two of Henry's toes. And Henry's hands have been burned so many times by bits of hot iron that they are as leathery as his apron.

The shoeing is done when Henry cuts off the end of each nail that has come through the wall, and twists the stub over to bury the sharp point. It's a perfect job.

As Henry leads Hannon back up the ramp, the forge fire smolders quietly. The police department will miss Henry next year. He is going to retire. Unknowingly, Hannon will miss him too. A good blacksmith who can give the perfect fit is a mighty good friend.

Henry.

Hannon and Mike cool off on a hot day.

Of course, the person whom Hannon would miss most of all would be Mike. According to mounted members, police horses "have been known to pine, lose weight from lack of appetite, and go into a physical decline when their riders retire or depart for other reasons." But chances are Hannon will retire before Mike, and they will work together until then. Most horses stay with the force for about fifteen years. Then they live on a farm in upstate New York where they have no work at all to do. For Hannon, it will be a return to his childhood days, when he did little else besides graze and play.

Officers, attached to their mounts after years of working together, often visit the retirement farm to see their old buddies. When Mike visits then, Hannon will probably still be a spirited horse, just a little less frisky.

But that is years away. Now Hannon is in the prime of his life, a hard-working horse on the streets of New York—a city horse.